EMMETT'S DREAM

Marylin Hafner

Cricket/McGraw-Hill

In memory of my sisters and brother.

"Molly and Emmett" appears monthly in *Ladybug*® magazine.
Visit our Web site at www.ladybugmag.com or call 1-800-827-0227
or write to *Ladybug* magazine, 315 Fifth Street, Peru, IL 61354.

Send all inquiries to:
McGraw-Hill Children's Publishing
8787 Orion Place
Columbus, OH 43240-4027

1-57768-896-1

1 2 3 4 5 6 7 8 9 10 PHXBK 07 06 05 04 03 02

Library of Congress Cataloging-in-Publication Data

Hafner, Marylin.
    Emmett's dream / by Marylin Hafner.
        p. cm.
    Summary: Molly gets so busy researching her family history for a school project that her cat Emmett feels left out, until Molly tells him about his own famous relatives. Includes suggestions for a genealogy project.
    ISBN 1-57768-896-1
    [1. Cats–Fiction. 2. Genealogy–Fiction. 3. Family–Fiction.]   I. Title.
    PZ7.H1198 Em 2002
    [E]–dc21
                                        2001005581

It was a bright, sunny day, but Molly was in her room.

Emmett helped Molly look through the old family picture albums and boxes of photos.

4

5

Emmett climbed up in his favorite tree to think. Molly was too busy to notice that he wasn't around.

7

8

That night Emmett could not sleep.

I WISH THERE WERE A STORY ABOUT MY LIFE.

LISTEN TO THIS, EMMETT!

AUNT KATIE WAS A WRITER.

AUNT SARA MADE THE BEST BIRTHDAY CAKES.

AUNT SYLVIA WAS A FASHION MODEL.

UNCLE LARRY WAS A FAMOUS MUSICIAN.

Molly told Emmett about some of his ancestors.

YOUR GREAT-GREAT-GREAT-GREAT-GREAT GRANDFATHER VISITED THE QUEEN AND FRIGHTENED ALL THE MICE OUT OF HER PALACE!

COOL!

And in ancient times, one of your ancestors helped build the pyramids.

Then when the Pilgrims came here, one of your
cousins was the first cat to step ashore!

18

It was a bright, moonlit night,
and Emmett fell asleep at once.

20

21

Emmett was glad to be home now! And look,
there was a note from Molly on the blanket.

WOW!
WHAT
A
DREAM!

Dear Em,
You were
asleep when
I left for
School.
See you
Later.
XX OO
MOLLY

That afternoon, Emmett waited for Molly at the school
bus stop.

Emmett was secretly glad that the story project was finished.

YOUR OWN STORY

FATHER'S FAMILY

MOTHER'S FAMILY

Your Family Tree

Get Mom or Dad to help you name some of your aunts and uncles and grandparents, too. How far up the tree can you go? Maybe the Internet can help you track down long-lost cousins by the dozens.

Every family tree looks different. Try making one of your own. Maybe your family stories are sprouting in all directions.

ARE YOU SURE UNCLE IRVING LIVED UP HERE, MOLLY?

Make a "story tree" with the names of all the people who have been special in your life.

1. Fill a flower pot with sand or soil.

2. Plant a "tree" using a fallen branch.

3. Write the names of everyone you love on tags and hang them on the branches.

28

COUSINS BY THE DOZENS

Story Scavenger Hunt

Ask family members in person, or phone or write to more distant relatives to find out memorable stories. Start with these questions or make up your own.

- What's the funniest thing you said when you were learning to talk?

- Who is your oldest living relative? The youngest? What do you have in common with that person?

- Where were you born? How did you get where you live now? Do you have a funny or exciting travel story?

You might want to make this a game. Have some friends ask their relatives the same questions. You can get together a week later and have fun comparing the answers.

Your Own Dream

Emmett didn't know about his family, so Molly helped him imagine links to famous ancestors. What figures from history would you choose to have in your family tree?

Can you help Emmett add to his list of famous felines? There's Puss-in-Boots . . . The Cheshire Cat . . . Dick Whittington's Cat . . . The Three Little Kittens. . . . You might find stories about them at the library.

SWEET DREAMS!

Marylin Hafner